Chloe and the Mermaid Club

A MERMAID GIRLS CHAPTER BOOK

A.M. Luzzader

ILLUSTRATED BY
CHADD VANZANTEN

Published by Knowledge Forest Press
P.O. Box 6331
Logan, UT 84341

Ebook ISBN-13: 978-1-949078-73-2
Paperback ISBN-13: 978-1-949078-72-5

Cover design by Beautiful Book Covers (beetifulbookcovers.com)

Editing by Chadd VanZanten

Interior illustrations by Chadd VanZanten

For every girl who dreams of mermaids

Contents

Chapter One

HAVE you ever wondered what it's like to live in the ocean? There are so many interesting and beautiful things for you to see!

Have you ever wondered what it would be like to always swim instead of walk? You would never have to touch the ground. It would feel like flying.

What about breathing water instead of air? Would you like that? If you don't like getting water in your nose, breathing water might be a little awkward.

This story is about a mermaid named Chloe Seawell. She had long, wavy, black hair. Her eyes were blue and her tail was a lovely pale green.

She breathed water, not air. She swam instead of walking. Chloe lived in the ocean.

And she loved it!

Chloe could swim in the ocean all day and never get bored. Sometimes she spent all day exploring the forests of tall, green kelp. Sometimes she swam along the beautiful coral reefs, watching the schools of brightly colored fish. Sometimes she dove down into the deep, undersea caves, where strange creatures lived.

She loved swimming fast! She zipped through the blue water and leaped over the waves, just like a dolphin.

On warm, summer days, Chloe sometimes did not swim at all. She just drifted through the water without moving her fins. The current and waves took her wherever they wanted.

Chloe loved the many kinds of fish who lived in the ocean. The angelfish swam slowly and were very pretty. They wore blue and yellow scales and long fins that trailed behind them in the water.

Then there were the long, silvery barracudas. They were hunter fish. Their eyes were alert and sharp. Their teeth were even sharper!

The porgy fish had spiny fins and scales of red and pink. They grouped together in schools of thousands and swam in the same direction. Then, they swam in a different direction, but always close together.

Clownfish did not swim in large schools. They hid themselves among the poisonous arms of sea anemones, but the poison did not harm them.

Merfolk were the guardians of the seas. They used mermagic to protect the ocean water and everything that lived in it. Merfolk learned mer-magical spells when they turned twelve years old. However, all merfolk knew a little mer-magic, such as how to make friends and be kind. That is a kind of magic.

Chloe was a very friendly mermaid. She made friends with tunas and sea turtles. She chatted with the talkative dolphins. She hung out with the giant clams, who never said a word. She even had a few friends who were grouchy old sharks. In fact, Chloe could make friends with practically anyone.

At school, Chloe learned about reading, math, and science. She would later learn more about mer-magic, but for now, she learned the basics. Chloe's favorite subject was art.

Chloe often got bored during math class and history class. She sometimes struggled with science class. Sometimes, when Chloe was supposed to be doing schoolwork, her teacher caught her doodling pictures on her worksheet. She drew sea flowers and snail shells. She drew oysters and cute little catfish.

Chloe loved to draw pictures of sea animals and plants, but she especially loved drawing portraits of merfolk. She loved drawing their faces and eyes. She loved to draw their hair and tail fins.

Almost everyone was a friend of Chloe. She sometimes had a hard time deciding who to spend time with. That's how she got the idea of forming a

Mermaid Club. With a club, she could invite everyone to do things together, because almost everyone was her friend.

The more Chloe thought about Mermaid Club, the more excited she became. Anyone who wanted to join could be a member. She wouldn't want anyone to feel left out. They would all help plan activities and projects. Best of all, they would do everything together.

Chloe told her parents about the idea for a club.

"Mermaid Club will be a group where merboys and mermaids can make new friends," said Chloe. "We will do fun activities, but we will also help to make the ocean a better place."

"It sounds wonderful, Chloe!" said her mother.

"That will be a fun group," said her father. "Good job!"

"The first thing I'll do is design a logo for the club," said Chloe.

A logo is a simple picture that stands for a group or company. Drawing a logo for Mermaid Club joined two of Chloe's favorite things—friends and artwork.

She gathered her art supplies and sat at the kitchen table. First, she drew a circle.

"I'm starting with a circle," said Chloe, "because

Mermaid Club will be like a circle. The circle will include anyone who wants to join."

Her parents smiled and nodded.

Inside the circle Chloe drew a bright blue mermaid tail splashing out of the water. She colored the background with yellow. In big, pink letters she wrote *Mermaid Club.*

"Your club logo looks very sharp!" said Chloe's mom.

"It's the perfect symbol for a club," said Chloe. "Tomorrow, I will invite other merkids to join!"

Chloe could hardly sleep that night. All she wanted to do was get to school and ask her classmates to join. She knew a lot of them would want to join. Maybe some people wouldn't want to, but that was okay. Everyone had to decide for themselves what they were interested in.

Chloe was happy when her two best friends, Emma Tailer and Ava Gillie, joined Mermaid Club.

Emma had wavy brown hair, brown eyes, and an orange tail. Emma was a bit shy, and she was much quieter than Chloe. Ava was a tall mermaid with a bluish-silver tail.

Chloe wanted lots more merkids in their club. The three friends would have to invite everyone. At the first official meeting of Mermaid Club, Chloe had been voted President. Ava was vice president, and Emma was secretary.

For their first activity, Mermaid Club visited the older merfolk at the Sunny Oceans Senior Living Center. That was fun. They got to know many of the residents there.

Next, they had a Mermaid Club square dance. Everyone had so much fun.

A few months later, Mermaid Club had more

than thirty-five members! Chloe, Ava, and Emma had invited every single merkid in their class. Some of them had joined. Some of them did not want to join Mermaid Club, but that was okay. Merkids from other classes wanted to join, too.

Mermaid Club was officially Chloe's favorite thing in the whole ocean! She couldn't wait until school was out each Friday, which is when Mermaid Club held their activities. The next planned activity was a visit to the yearly sand sculpture contest.

This will be a very fun activity, thought Chloe. *I am excited to see all the different sand sculptures.*

Chloe didn't know it yet, but the next activity was actually going to be a little upsetting for her.

THE MERMAID CLUB members met at the Happy Sands Park. That was where the sand sculpture contest was held.

"Thanks for coming, everyone," said Chloe. "I am happy to report that we now have almost forty members! We have lots of activities planned. In two weeks we will do a litter clean-up around North Beach. We will also take a class on first aid. Those are important activities, but today's activity is just for fun. I hope you all enjoy it."

The other Mermaid Club members clapped and cheered.

The sand sculpting contest was an annual event, which means it happened every year. Merfolk from all over the ocean would gather at Happy Sands Park and spend many hours molding and sculpting the sand into castles, giant fish, ships, and other shapes. All the visitors would vote on the sculptures they thought were the best. Then, the judges of the contest would count the votes and name the winners. There were trophies and prizes.

Chloe loved the sand sculpture contest. She never missed it. That's why she suggested this activity to the Mermaid Club. It combined the two things she loved the most: art and Mermaid Club!

There was a merman with Chloe. She turned to him and said, "Everyone, this is Mr. Abalone. He works here at the park. He's in charge of the sand sculpture contest, and he has a few words to say to us."

"Hello, merkids," said Mr. Abalone. He was a short merman who wore glasses and held a clipboard. His tail was dark red. He had a kind face and a friendly smile. "I would like to welcome you to the Happy Sands Park Sculpture Contest. I'm so glad you're here. We have booklets for each of you. I hope you enjoy the sculptures!"

All the members of Mermaid Club would visit the sand sculptures in teams of two. They could look at all the sand sculptures and then vote for the ones they liked best. Afterwards, yummy treats would be served. Chloe's mom had baked a big batch of seanut-butter cookies.

Chloe helped everyone to find a partner. She was careful to make sure no one was left out. She knew that sometimes some of her friends were a little bit bashful. Some friends would be embarrassed trying to find a partner. Emma was that way. Sometimes she was embarrassed about speaking up. This wasn't a bad thing, but Chloe did not want anyone to be left out or forgotten. That is why Chloe asked Emma to be her partner.

"Oh, yes," said Emma. "I was hoping I could be your partner, Chloe!"

Chloe and Emma helped everyone find a partner.

Chloe swam over to Jack Mackerel. "Jack," she said, "why don't you go with Sammy Sails."

"Okay," said Jack. "We'll make a great team."

Emma asked Jillian Seagull if she would like to be Tim Kelper's partner.

"Yes," said Jillian. "Tim's nice. I like him."

After making sure everyone had a partner, Chloe said, "Okay, teams. You have two hours to go and see all the sand sculptures. Look at the sculptures and vote for your favorites. Then meet back here at 6 o'clock!"

"Shall we go and see the sculptures, Chloe?" said Emma.

"Yes!" said Chloe. "Let's go!"

They picked up their booklets from Mr. Abalone. Emma and Chloe looked at the booklets as they swam to the sculptures. The booklets had information about the sculptures and artists. There were also pages to mark down your favorite sculptures.

"Wow," said Chloe, "it says here that they have to bring in extra sand for the contest."

"That's amazing," said Emma, reading her booklet. "Hey, it says that this year's theme is mythical creatures."

This meant that all the creatures would be from fairy tales and fantasy stories, like unicorns, elves, or dragons.

"Oh, that's cool!" said Chloe. "I can't wait to see them all."

Chloe and Emma walked around the park. The sand artists stood by their creations. They waved at the visitors as they came to see their sand sculptures.

First Emma and Chloe came to a giant sea serpent. It was very long and the artists had carved sharp scales on its skin. It had huge teeth and a long tongue.

"Whoa," said Emma. "It almost looks real!"

"Yeah!" cried Chloe. "It's incredible!"

Next, they came to a sand sculpture of another mythical creature, a unicorn. It had a flowing mane, a long tail, and a spiral horn on its head.

"That one's very pretty!" said Chloe, pointing at the unicorn.

"Yes, I like it, too," said Emma.

The next sculpture they came to was an elephant. Elephants are real, as you know. They are not mythical or magical.

However, the merfolk did not know that. You may have even seen a real elephant. The merfolk had never really been on land, and so they'd never seen a real elephant. So, the merfolk weren't sure if elephants were real or not. They thought that elephants had six legs, too. That is how many legs the sand sculpture elephant had.

Chloe and Emma looked at the elephant sculpture.

"It's so huge!" said Chloe. "Look at its long nose and tusks."

"I love the wrinkly skin and its big ears," said Emma.

There was also a sand sculpture kangaroo. You know that kangaroos are real, but the merfolk did not. They were also not sure if kangaroos had wings. So, they put wings on their kangaroo sand sculpture, just to be safe. Everyone agreed that the sand sculpture looked pretty good.

"Look at the kangaroo!" said Chloe. "The wings are amazing!"

All the sculptures were beautiful. Chloe knew that the sand artists must have spent hours and hours on their creations. They were very skilled. Chloe was very impressed. After an hour or so, Chloe and Emma had seen all the sculptures. Chloe had made some notes in her booklet.

"Wasn't that so incredible?" said Emma. "I really loved them all."

"Me too," said Chloe, flipping through her booklet. "But we have to pick our favorite to vote for. Which one was your favorite?"

"Either the unicorn or the kangaroo," said Emma.

"Those were really well done," said Chloe. "I especially liked the detail on the kangaroo wings."

"Which sand sculpture did you like best?" asked Emma.

"Definitely the sea serpent," said Chloe. "The way it curved back and forth and was so long. It was awesome! I'd like to go back and take a picture of it."

Chloe and Emma swam back to the area where the sea serpent sculpture was. Because it was almost time for the park to close, the area was almost empty. The sand artists had left the park, because it was getting dark. They were gathered at the rec center for the awards ceremony.

"Perfect!" said Chloe. "No one else is here, so I can get a good picture!"

Chloe got out her camera to take a picture, but the sea serpent was so long she couldn't fit it all in the frame.

"Hang on," she said. "I have to back up."

She kept swimming backwards while looking into her camera.

"Almost got it," she said, backing up some more. She pushed the button and took the picture. She looked at the camera. It was a really good photo! Chloe had moved back far enough to get the entire sea serpent in the frame. It looked great. But then Chloe bumped into something behind her.

"Look out!" said Emma.

It was too late. Chloe had accidentally backed into one of the other sculptures. It was the dragon, which was one of the tallest sculptures. The dragon sculpture stood on its back legs. It had a long neck and huge wings.

Chloe only bumped into the dragon's cheek, but sand sculptures are very delicate.

The dragon's neck tipped over and broke the sea serpent! The sea serpent tipped over and hit the nearby gnome sand sculpture. The gnome's tall hat tipped over and bumped into the elephant. The elephant fell over and crashed into the kangaroo.

This went on until half the sculptures in the park had been knocked over or damaged.

It was a disaster!

Chapter Three

"Oh no," cried Chloe.

She swam over to the sand sculptures, but it was too late. So many of the sand sculptures were completely gone. So much time and effort, all ruined. Chloe felt shocked.

Emma came swimming over. She covered her mouth with her hands.

"What should I do?" asked Chloe.

"I don't know," said Emma.

"Maybe I can fix it," said Chloe.

She dug around in the sand, trying to pile it back up. Emma tried to help. However, no matter how they pressed the sand together, it just fell apart. It was no use.

Chloe's heart pounded. "Emma, it's not going to work! What should I do?"

"We should probably go tell someone," said Emma.

"I can't do that!" said Chloe. "I don't want anyone to know it was my fault. I'm so embarrassed. Maybe no one will notice."

Just then, Ava and Nevaeh swam up to Chloe and Emma. Ava gasped. Nevaeh's eyes were wide with shock.

"What happened to all the sand sculptures?" Ava asked.

Chloe's cheeks burned. "Uh, what do you mean?"

"The dragon! The elephant! The gnome! They've all been destroyed!" cried Nevaeh.

"I'm not sure!" said Chloe.

She didn't know what else to do or say. She quickly swam away. Emma followed.

"Wait," called Emma, trying to catch up with Chloe. "Where are we going?"

But Chloe wouldn't stop, she zipped and darted through the park. When she was out of sight of her friends, she hid in the nearby coral reef.

It would soon be time for the Mermaid Club to

gather again and talk about the activity. That was the last thing Chloe wanted to do.

She thought, *I wish Mermaid Club had never come to the sand sculpting contest. In fact, I wish I'd never thought of the Mermaid Club.*

Chloe knew that Emma or Ava had probably told the sand sculpture artists what had happened. *Everyone will know I ruined the sand sculptures. It'll be so embarrassing having to face everyone.*

Chloe loved her friends. She loved spending time with mermaids and merboys. She loved Mermaid Club. But now all she wanted to do was go home and hide. She wanted to be alone. Chloe knew she should tell the people at the sand sculpture contest what she'd done. It would be very embarrassing. And it would be embarrassing to tell the others in the Mermaid Club. And so she stayed hidden in the coral reef.

Chloe couldn't explain why, but she felt sick thinking about what had happened. She felt as if she had eaten some bad squid or a spoiled sardine casserole. All she could think about was how awesome the sculptures had been—until she ruined it all with her carelessness.

Maybe I can just wait, thought Chloe. *I'll wait*

until everyone in Mermaid Club has gone home. Then I'll go back to the park and talk to the sand sculpture artists. I'll tell them what happened. It will be so embarrassing, but maybe they'll understand.

Chloe waited a long time in her hiding place among the coral. Then she heard someone calling her name.

"Chloe?" called the voice. "Chloe, are you here somewhere?"

Then Chloe recognized the voice. It was Emma.

Chapter Four

FROM HER HIDING place in the coral, Chloe watched as Emma swam by, calling her name.

"Chloe? Chloe!"

Ava was with Emma. They were both looking for her. And they were coming closer to Chloe, so Chloe swam away and found another place to hide.

"Hey, what was that?" said Ava. "I saw something over there."

Emma followed Ava. "Chloe?" they said. "Is that you?"

Chloe knew they were going to find her. She swam to another place to hide.

"Someone's over there!" said Emma. "Follow me."

Emma and Ava swam under the coral reef and

above it. They swam this way and that. There were lots of hiding places in the coral reef. There were caverns and crevices. Every time Ava and Emma got close, Chloe swam to a new hiding place.

"Chloe?" said Ava. "Is that you? Are you hiding?"

"Come out and talk to us," said Emma.

"Yeah," added Ava. "We're just gonna keep looking for you."

Chloe finally sighed and swam out from her

hiding spot. "You don't need to keep looking for me," said Chloe. "I'm right here."

"Why were you hiding?" asked Ava.

"I'm ashamed that I ruined the sand sculptures," said Chloe. She began to cry.

"It was an accident," said Emma. "We just need to go tell someone in charge. They will wonder what happened."

"I know," said Chloe. "I'm just so embarrassed. I don't want to see anyone right now because I feel bad."

"I know what it's like to be embarrassed, and I know it's not fun," said Ava.

"You do?" Chloe asked.

"Sure," said Ava. "Everyone gets embarrassed sometimes."

Emma nodded and said, "When I was a little merkid, I was at a supermarket with my mom. I wanted to show her a sandy bar that I wanted for a treat. I grabbed her hand and began to pull her toward the shelf where the sandy bars were."

"Why is that so embarrassing?" asked Chloe, sniffing away her tears. "I love sandy bars."

"Because it wasn't my mom's hand!" replied Emma. "I had grabbed a stranger's hand instead! I was so embarrassed I almost cried."

"Oh, dear," said Chloe. "That is embarrassing. But kind of funny, too."

"Yeah," said Emma. "I can laugh about it now, but it was terrible at the time."

Ava said, "One day at school last year, Jay Wavey asked me what I thought about Mrs. Crest."

"The P.E. teacher at school?" asked Chloe.

"Yes," said Ava. "I told Jay I didn't like Mrs. Crest

very much because she yells at everyone in class. I called her a sea grouch."

"That doesn't sound very embarrassing," said Chloe. "Mrs. Crest really does yell a lot."

"Yes," said Ava, "but then Jay told me that Mrs. Crest is his aunt!"

"Oh, no," said Chloe, putting her face into her hand. "That's very embarrassing! Was Jay Wavey angry at you?"

"No," said Ava. "He said he knew that Mrs. Crest yells a lot. But I still wanted to crawl under a rock and stay there forever."

Chloe smiled and wiped away the last of her mermaid tears. Hearing that her friends sometimes had embarrassing moments helped her to feel better. It reminded her that she had had other embarrassing moments. Last summer, Chloe had tripped on a giant stingray and spilled a seaberry kelp shake all down the front of her favorite jacket. Chloe went home very embarrassed. But she hardly thought about it anymore, and she knew it wasn't really that serious or bad. And there were other embarrassing moments, too. She had forgotten all about them.

But this time, she'd ruined the work of other people. The sand sculpture people had worked hard on their creations.

"I know I should go talk to the sand sculpture artists," said Chloe, "but I don't want anyone to see me. I still feel very bad about what happened. I'm worried they will be angry at me. I'm afraid they will scold me."

"I don't know what will happen," said Emma, "but you can't just hide out here in the coral reef for the rest of the day."

"Yeah," said Chloe. "You're right."

Ava said, "I have an idea!"

"What is it?" asked Chloe.

"We'll come with you!" said Ava. "That way, you won't have to be alone."

This was a little bit of mermagic that all merfolk knew about. When there was something difficult to do, they stayed together to support each other. Being in a group of friends or family always made everything easier. It was friendship magic.

"Oh, I think that will make me feel better," said Chloe. "Yes, will you both please come with me? I can do it if you come with me."

"Yes," said Emma. "Of course we will come with

you. And I think that someday, we will be able to laugh at this embarrassing story, too."

"I don't know about that," said Chloe. "I knocked over so many sand sculptures."

"You might be surprised," said Ava. "I bet everyone in the Mermaid Club has a pretty good embarrassing story."

Chloe still didn't want to go and tell the sand sculpture merfolk what happened. But she knew she must do it. And she felt a little better because of Ava and Emma's friendship magic.

"Okay," she said to Emma and Ava. "Let's go, and I will tell the sand sculpture people what happened."

Ava and Emma each held one of Chloe's hands, and together they swam away.

Chapter Five

The three mermaid friends swam into the park. They could see the piles of sand where many of the sand sculptures used to be.

"The sand sculptures were so beautiful and interesting," said Chloe. "And then I wrecked them."

"It was an accident," said Emma. "Accidents happen."

"Do you think the sand artists will be angry at me?" asked Chloe.

"I don't know," said Ava. "I hope not."

"Do you think they will yell at me?" asked Chloe.

"I'm not sure," said Emma. "I hope they won't."

In the middle of the park, there was an area with tables and chairs. All the sand sculpture artists were there, along with Mr. Abalone. They were having a meeting. Chloe, Ava, and Emma swam toward them. As they got closer, they could hear what the merfolk were saying.

"I am so angry!" said one of the sand sculpture artists. She was a tall mermaid with blonde hair, green eyes, and bright blue tail fins. She was a college student named Selma Iceberg. "Why would someone destroy our work? That was a mean thing to do."

Some of the other sand artists agreed. "Yes," they said. "It was a terrible thing to do."

"Well," said another artist, "the contest was already over. Also, sand sculptures never last forever. The tides and currents always break them down after a few days."

"Yes," said Selma, "but someone wrecked our sculptures for no reason!"

Chloe was nervous. Some of the artists were angry after all. Chloe was afraid they would yell at her or scold her. But Emma and Ava were right—Chloe must tell the artists what she did.

Choe took a few deep breaths. She slowly breathed in the cool ocean water. This was another mer-magical trick that all merfolk knew. Taking a deep breath always made merfolk feel a little calmer. Chloe breathed in slowly, held it, then she breathed out. The mermagic calmed her down.

"Excuse me," said Chloe. "Hello."

She swam forward. The merfolk from the park looked at Chloe. The sand artists looked at Chloe. Mr. Abalone and Selma looked at Chloe.

"Hi, Chloe," said Mr. Abalone. "I was just collecting the votes from the contest and getting ready for the awards ceremony. However, something awful has happened. Somebody knocked over many of the sculptures!"

"Yes, I know," said Chloe.

"Ah, you saw who ruined the sculptures?" asked Mr. Abalone.

"Yes," said Chloe, "but that's not what I meant. What I meant to say is that I'm the one who ruined the sculptures."

"You?" said Mr. Abalone. "You did this?"

Selma seemed very angry. "Why did you do that?" she said. "Why did you ruin our work?"

Now everyone was looking at Chloe. They were waiting for her answer.

"I'm so sorry!" cried Chloe. "I didn't mean to do it! It was an accident!"

"An accident?" asked Mr. Abalone.

"Yes," said Chloe. "I bumped into the dragon. It tipped over and broke the sea serpent. Then the sea serpent fell over onto the gnome. The gnome's hat crashed into the elephant, and the elephant tipped over onto the kangaroo!"

"It's true," said Emma. "I was with her. She was trying to take a picture. It really was an accident."

"I'm very sorry," said Chloe. "Your sculptures were all so beautiful! I love the sand sculpture contest.

I come to see it every year. I would never ruin any of your sculptures on purpose."

"Thank you for telling us, Chloe," said Selma. She didn't seem so angry anymore. "We thought someone had broken up the sculptures just to be cruel."

"You're not angry?" asked Chloe.

"Well," said Selma, "not really. The contest was already over. And we all know that sand sculptures don't last forever. They would probably start crumbling tomorrow. But I was so busy this year, I didn't get a chance to take a picture of my sculpture, and I am sad about that. I was angry a moment ago, but not anymore."

"Oh, I'm so sorry," Chloe said again. "Yes, that's sad. Which sculpture was yours?"

"The sea serpent," said Selma.

"The sea serpent?" said Chloe, her face suddenly bright. "That was my favorite! I took a picture of it just before the accident! I can give you a copy of it!"

"That's wonderful!" cried Selma. "Can you show it to me? Can I see it?"

"Of course!" said Chloe.

She took the camera from her backpack and turned it on. Selma joined her and looked at the photo.

"That's a great picture!" said Selma. "What a relief! I'm so happy. I'm glad everything worked out."

"I apologize again for ruining the sculptures," Chloe said to the artists and to Mr. Abalone. "All of the sculptures were so amazing and fun to see. I thought you would scold me and make me feel dumb."

Mr. Abalone shook his head and smiled. "Accidents happen. You did the right thing, Chloe. All of the artists thought that someone knocked down the sculptures to be mean. If you had not told us, their feelings would be hurt."

"Yes," said one of the other artists. "Thank you for telling us. You don't have to feel embarrassed. We have all done things like that."

"You have?" asked Chloe.

"Oh, yes," said one of the artists. "I'm an art teacher. One day I taught a whole day of classes with a huge smudge of pink paint on my forehead!"

Everyone chuckled at this.

"I was so embarrassed at the time," said the artist, "but now it's funny."

Mr. Abalone took the pen from his clipboard and made a note on his paper. "I am going to make a policy for next year's contest. All the sculptures must be more spread out. That way, if one of them falls down, it won't fall on any others."

"Good idea, Mr. Abalone," said Selma.

"How embarrassing!" said Chloe, putting her face into her hands.

Emma and Ava smiled and laughed quietly.

"Why are you laughing?" said Chloe.

"Well," said Ava, "you have to admit it's kind of funny. Mr. Abalone had to make a whole new rule for the Happy Sands Sculpture Contest just because of you!"

Chloe's face turned red, but she laughed softly. "Yeah," she said. "I guess it is a little funny."

Selma, Mr. Abalone, and the other sand artists laughed, too, but in a friendly way. Chloe's embarrassing moment happened only about an hour ago, but it was already turning into a funny thing. Chloe shook her head and laughed a little louder.

"And now that we have cleared up all the trouble," said Mr. Abalone, "let's all go to the rec center for the awards ceremony!"

Chapter Six

Chloe, Emma, and Ava swam to the rec center for the awards ceremony. It was a large cavern located at the center of the park. Lots of the members of Mermaid Club came along, too.

Inside the rec center, a slideshow was projected onto a large screen. It was a slideshow of all the contest winners from past years. There was a picture of the large whale sculpture that won first place last year. And there was a picture of a giant squid sculpture, which won first place the year before that. One of the slides was a photo of a handsome pirate sculpture that had won the contest more than ten years ago.

Ava, Emma, and Chloe found some seats and

watched the slideshow. There were many incredible sculptures to see.

As they watched the slideshow, Chloe turned to her friends and said, "Thank you for helping me today. I'm so glad you're my friends."

"No problem," said Ava, patting Chloe on the back. "You would have done the same for us."

"Yeah," said Ava. "It takes guts to admit when

you've made a mistake, even when it's just an accident."

Chloe hoped she never did something so embarrassing ever again. However, she knew she might someday. She knew embarrassing things just happen now and then. They are hard to control.

When everyone had a seat in the rec center, Mr. Abalone went to the front of the room. He signaled someone to turn off the slideshow.

"Welcome to the awards ceremony for the Happy Sands Sculpture Contest," said Mr. Abalone. "We saw some outstanding sculptures this year!"

The crowd agreed by cheering and clapping their hands.

"Congratulations to all the artists. You have all put on a great show! My staff has counted all the votes," said Mr. Abalone, "and I will now announce this year's winners."

Everyone chattered with excitement.

"In third place," said Mr. Abalone, "is the Kangaroo with Wings, by Ricky Bluewater and his team of talented artists. This is the first year Ricky Bluewater's has been in the contest. Congratulations to them!"

Everyone applauded and cheered. Ricky Bluewater and his team came up to the front of the room. Mr. Abalone gave them the third-place trophy.

"In second place," said Mr. Abalone, "is the Gnome with The Tall Hat, by Julia Typhoon and her incredible team of artists. This is the first time Julia's team has won a trophy in the contest. Let's hear it for them!"

Again, everyone clapped and cheered. Julia Typhoon and her team came to the front of the room. Mr. Abalone gave them the second-place trophy.

"And now," said Mr. Abalone, "I will announce this year's first place winner. It is Giant Sea Serpent, by Selma Iceberg and her team!"

Chloe applauded the loudest. Selma's sea serpent was her favorite sculpture that year. Selma and her team of artists went up to the front of the room. Mr. Abalone gave them the big first place trophy.

When Selma and her sand artists had taken their seats again, Mr. Abalone said, "I want to tell you something else. As you know, there was a mishap this year, and some of the sculptures were ruined."

Why he is talking about this? thought Chloe. *Is he going to tell everyone that I ruined the sculptures? Haven't I had enough embarrassment?*

"Selma Iceberg did not get a chance to take a

photo of her team's big sea serpent sculpture," said Mr. Abalone. "This was very sad."

Chloe kept listening. She was very nervous now.

"Luckily for us," said Mr. Abalone, "Chloe Seawell, the president of the Mermaid Club, was here at the contest this year. She took a picture of the sea serpent. It's a lovely photo, and we have already added it to our slideshow."

He signaled for the picture to be shown on the screen.

Chloe's photo of the sea serpent appeared on the screen. The photo showed the scales on the sea serpent's body and the sharp teeth in its mouth. Everyone said, "Ooo," and "Ahh." And then they clapped. A big grin appeared on Chloe's face.

"And one last thing," said Mr. Abalone. "I have set a new policy for next year's contest."

Oh, no! thought Chloe. The grin on her face vanished. She knew about Mr. Abalone's new policy. He had to make it just for her. The new policy was that the sculptures would be spread out so that no one could knock them all down at the same time. Chloe admitted that it was kind of funny. But she didn't want everyone in the rec center to know she was the one who knocked over the sculptures.

Chloe looked at Emma and Ava. Their eyes were large, and they looked worried, too. They didn't want Chloe to be embarrassed again.

"The new policy," said Mr. Abalone, "is that we will have a special photographer take pictures of every single sculpture, as soon as it is finished. Sometimes the sand artists are very busy. They forget to take pictures. Or the sculptures get damaged. This way, we will always have nice pictures of all the sculptures."

"Oh, whew," said Chloe.

Ava and Emma giggled softly.

Chloe's face had turned red again, but she laughed, too.

Please leave a review

Thank you for reading this book. I hope you enjoyed it! I would really appreciate it if you would please take a moment to review Chloe and the Mermaid Club at the retail site where it was purchased. This helps me to reach new readers. Thank you!

—A.M. Luzzader

WWW.AMLUZZADER.COM

- blog
- freebies
- newsletter
- contact info

About the Author

A.M. Luzzader is an award-winning children's book author who writes chapter books and middle grade books. She specializes in writing books for preteens including *A Mermaid in Middle Grade and Arthur Blackwood's Scary Stories for Kids who Like Scary Stories*

A.M. decided she wanted to write fun stories for

kids when she was still a kid herself. By the time she was in fourth grade, she was already writing short stories. In fifth grade, she bought a typewriter at a garage sale to put her words into print, and in sixth grade she added illustrations.

Now that she has decided what she wants to be when she grows up, A.M. writes books for kids full time. She was selected as the Writer of the Year in 2019-2020 by the League of Utah Writers.

A.M. is the mother of a 12-year-old and a 15-year-old who often inspire her stories. She lives with her husband and children in northern Utah. She is a devout cat person and avid reader.

A.M. Luzzader's books are appropriate for ages 5-12. Her chapter books are intended for kindergarten to third grade, and her middle grade books are for third grade through sixth grade. Find out more about A.M., sign up to receive her newsletter, and get special offers at her website: www.amluzzader.com.

OTHER BOOKS BY

A.M. Luzzader

Mermaid Club: A mermaid girls chapter book

For ages 6-10

OTHER BOOKS BY

A.M. Luzzader

A Fairy Tale Chapter Book Series for Kids

For ages 6-10

OTHER BOOKS BY

A.M. Luzzader

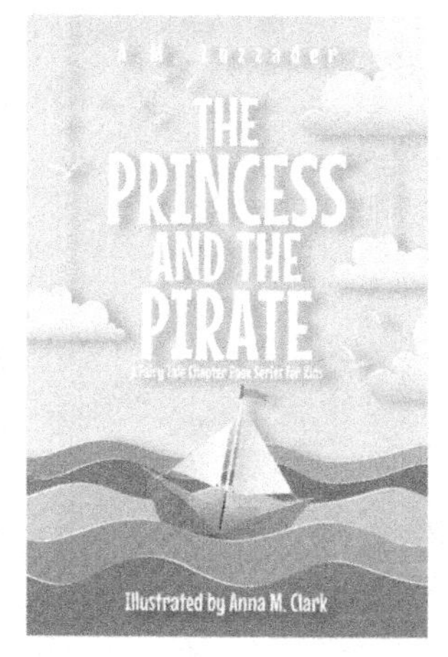

A Fairy Tale Chapter Book Series for Kids

For ages 6-10

OTHER BOOKS BY

A.M. Luzzader

A Magic School for Girls
Chapter Book

For ages
6-8

OTHER BOOKS BY

A.M. Luzzader

Decker's Video Game Rescue Agency

For ages 6-10

OTHER BOOKS BY

A.M. Luzzader

A Mermaid in Middle Grade

Books 1–3

For ages 8-12

OTHER BOOKS BY

A.M. Luzzader

A Mermaid in Middle Grade
Books 4–6

For ages
8-12

OTHER BOOKS BY
A.M. Luzzader

Hannah Saves the World

Books 1-3

For ages
8-12

Made in the USA
Coppell, TX
08 October 2023